CURIOUSER AND CURIOUSER

Flash Fiction

By

TONY DAWSON

Table of Contents

The Grave's a Fine and Private Place....................................3

The Snuffing Machine....................................7

The Hereafter....................................12

Cats and Dogs....................................14

Death of a Plumber....................................16

The Dwarf Part I....................................20

The Dwarf Part II....................................23

The Irony of Noir....................................26

HRT....................................29

Daisies and Mallows....................................31

Homophone....................................33

Home Sweet Home....................................35

Extraordinary General Meeting of the Four Horsemen of the Apocalypse....................................38

Shogun....................................43

Acknowledgements....................................49

The Grave's a Fine and Private Place

Clutching my holdall, I slipped into the chantry of an early fifteenth-century chapel. It was late at night, and the only light in the chapel was provided by half a dozen flickering candles that created disturbing shadows on the walls. I was interested in the tomb of a medieval knight and his lady and although I had never felt comfortable in the presence of death, even in the daylight hours, if I had come during the day, I would have been spotted by the sacristan and asked to leave.

Brass rubbings, the reason for my clandestine visit, had been banned by the church, but I was determined to make a rubbing of the diminutive medieval knight armiger, William, and his even more diminutive wife, Adela. Married in 1381, she had died in 1414, he in 1420 and they lay side by side in the table tomb that I could dimly see in front of me. The extraordinary brass bas relief effigies of the couple occupied the top of their tomb. Stale incense lingered in the air but was not sufficient to eliminate the damp musty smell of that ancient chapel. I shivered.

After peering around in the semi-darkness to check that I was alone, I took out a roll of paper, spread it over the image of Adela and carefully taped it down to ensure it stayed in place when I started the rubbing. Beginning with her headdress and noble features, I was delighted to see how well she was emerging on the paper. As I moved down, her hands held in prayer proved a little tricky because of the way the sleeves of her gown covered her knuckles and it wasn't easy to see detail in the baleful light, but I eventually achieved a satisfactory reproduction. Then, as I passed the heelball over her hips, I thought I heard a little sigh of pleasure…but that was impossible, surely. I must have imagined it. Nevertheless, as the heelball began to work on the crotch area of her close kirtle, I distinctly heard a squeal of delight followed by a little moan. The hair on the back of my neck stood on end. I paused for a moment, holding my breath, my ear cocked. Silence. I hastily moved on to the hem of her dress and the effigy of the dog at her feet. At least, it didn't bark!

Having finished the rubbing of the knight's wife, I peeled away the tape and the paper, thinking all the time about those sounds of sensual pleasure. Did rubbing the brass cause static electricity, sending a little stimulus into the next world? Was I acting as some kind of Ouija board vibrator between now and the hereafter? What an idea! The atmosphere was obviously affecting me. Putting such ridiculous thoughts out of my mind, I taped the brass rubbing paper over the effigy of the diminutive knight armiger who was clad in spectacular full plate armour. I was particularly keen to ensure that the details of the bascinet with its enriched edging and high gorget, the breastplates and palettes at the shoulders were captured in the rubbing. Having achieved that to my satisfaction, I began to work on his skirt of tassets, cuisses, and jambs. Just when I began to apply the heelball vigorously between the cuisses and the jambs, I heard a man's deep moan of pleasure echoing round the chantry! I marvelled at the sound. What was going on? My trembling fingers dropped the heelball, which rolled away into the darkness. With the knight's rubbing only half finished, I scrambled to pack up my belongings and made a beeline for the exit. And that was when, through the gloom, I caught sight of the sacristan, his cassock hoisted above his waist, pulling on some shorts as he emerged from a confessional in the far corner of the chapel. As he hurried away a plump woman, possibly a parishioner, staggered out of the same confessional, busily adjusting her clothing, and followed him through a nearby door into the grounds of the church. "Well, **she** was certainly no coy mistress," I thought. "It seems that I wasn't the only one engaged in some rubbing!" And Andrew Marvell was right after all: the grave **is** a fine and private place, but none, I think, do there embrace and it was simply my fevered imagination that had been playing tricks on me! Pity about the knight's rubbing, though…

The Snuffing Machine

Summer jobs, eh, don't you just love 'em? At the end of the 1950s during a university vacation, I found a summer job at a jam factory on the outskirts of a northern industrial city. The first fellow-worker I met was operating a machine that topped and tailed gooseberries that were to be bottled. It was called a snuffing machine. The man operating it looked as if he was quite capable of snuffing or topping more than just gooseberries …

Kevin was in his mid-30s, about my height but built like a brick shithouse. His shoulders sloped from his thick neck like the sides of the Matterhorn. His thinning hair was sandy-coloured. The glint in his eye, the lopsided grin, and cocky posture told the world that nothing much mattered to him. That he could face down anybody.

However, I immediately piqued his interest. He had sussed out at once that I was "a student" but he couldn't quite understand how this skinny young man from *a working-class* family was studying at the local university. In those far off days, university students from my background were as thin on the ground as the hair on his head. He quizzed me on what sort of degree I was doing (Languages), where I was from (London) and what plans I had for the future (teaching, what else?).

During our first tea break, we continued our chat.

"I'm looking for a cheap flat locally," I ventured, "I'm fed up with living in lodgings."

"Well, it so happens that there's an empty flat next to mine," he replied. "I can show it to you after work if you like."

The building he lived in was a large, Victorian, terraced house converted into a number of cheap, tatty flats. Naïve as I was, I expected him to call the owner to show me around, but he simply opened the door with the dexterity of a practised burglar and let me in. It consisted of one large room that was bare except for a ramshackle table and a couple of sit-up-and-beg chairs. In one corner there was a rusty, antediluvian gas stove that looked like a potential death-trap. An added feature of this bijou residence was the wallpaper peeling off the damp walls. The grimy bathroom, on the same floor, was shared with the other tenants and doubtless a thousand cockroaches. Kevin proceeded to give me the landlord's telephone number and since the rent was well within my budget, even by the standards of a poverty-stricken student, I signed up at once and moved in after buying a secondhand hospital bed and mattress through Kevin's connections.

My new friend and neighbour, who lived with a woman he always referred to as his "bird", turned out to have a colourful, not to say arresting, past.

"I like to move around," he chuckled, "Partly because I get bored shitless if I have to do the same thing for very long and partly because I've had a few run-ins with the law." Now, that didn't surprise me!

His contact with the law was reflected in the way he spoke: an odd mixture of colloquialisms and obscenities larded with legal jargon that he'd picked up over the years while standing before prosecutors, magistrates, and judges.

"Before I started work at the jam factory, I had a labouring job on a building site and for some reason I never quite fathomed, the foreman took a dislike to me," he grinned, "The bugger never stopped needling me."

In those days, a foreman on a building site had total power over those under him. He could terminate a labourer's employment on a whim, without explanation, notice, or compensation.

"One day, the miserable sod decided to sack me for no reason" said Kevin indignantly, "and I got angry and told him what I thought of him. The foreman grabbed a shovel and came at me, so I punched his lights out, no problem!"

"Didn't that put you in danger of prosecution, and being sent to prison?"

He laughed and said, "Nah, because the foreman '*had offered violence and thereby*' fucked himself!"

"Anyway, that was nothing," Kevin muttered, "considering that I have actually killed someone..."

I could feel the blood draining from my face. Kevin could see I was aghast.

"Well, he was trying to touch me up, for Christ's sake!" he spluttered, as if I would understand. "I ended up being sentenced to 5 years in the slammer for manslaughter."

"How come you got off so lightly for actually killing someone?"

He gave me his lopsided grin, "Easy. I had a bloody good lawyer, that's why, and he told me to plead the 'Portsmouth defence', so I did."

Evidently, the "Portsmouth defence" referred to in Kevin's parlance was also known as the "Guardsman's defence", and more recently as "the gay panic defence". It was a legal stratagem employed by defence lawyers in cases where the defendant had felt threatened by a homosexual approaching him for what until well into the 1960s was an illegal sexual act. The use of violence against a homosexual in such circumstances, even if it culminated in his death, was considered legitimate defence. Such a line obviously appealed to bigoted jurors of the day and while not quite a "get-out-of-jail-free" card, it came pretty close. It certainly meant avoiding the death penalty, as in Kevin's case.

And that's how I came to know Kevin, the snuffing machine… but just to be on the safe side, I was quick to show him pictures of the girl I planned to marry. I didn't want him to feel "threatened"!

The Hereafter

After the party at the frat house, the president of Beta Psi hooked up with one of the waitresses employed by the caterers, and who happened to be British. He just loved the sound of her accent, not to mention her curves. Having enticed the girl into his car, he drove twenty miles to a secluded spot. Once they had arrived and he had killed the engine, he turned to her and slid his hand up her skirt.

"Let's consider the Hereafter," he said, with a frat boy laugh, as he unzipped his fly with the other hand. "Because if you're not here after what I'm here after," he sniggered "then you'll be here after I drive away!" (In his head he was singing "I'm so pretty, I'm so pretty, and witty and bright and I pity any girl who isn't here with me tonight".)

The waitress gave him a knowing wink.

"Just hang on a minute while I look for my contraceptive device." She was smiling shyly as she rummaged in her purse.

"Oh, sure," said the smirking frat boy.

Before he knew it, she had pulled out her device, a Smith and Wesson Lady Smith 357, and shot his balls off there and then. It was such a remote spot that nobody could hear his screams. The resourceful waitress kicked him out of the car so that he would bleed out on the grass. She then grabbed a towel that was on the back seat—the frat boy had come well prepared—and placed it carefully over the blood on the driver's seat and slid across to sit on it. There, she adjusted the seat so that she could reach the accelerator and the brake pedal and once she was comfortable, yelled at the frat boy through the window,

"Honey, I just whipped your ass as you Americans like to say. *You're* the one who'll be here after *I've* driven away, and it won't be long before it's you that's in the *real* Hereafter."

She revved the engine and as she prepared to drive off into the night, called out to him:

"You ought to know, given what you're paying for your education, that 'yank' is synonymous with 'jerk'. But in England you'd probably be called a 'berk'.

Cats and Dogs

Mark lay back in the warm bath, eyes shut, the water soothing his aching limbs. Dozy, still convalescing from a severe bout of flu, mind wandering, and conjuring up all sorts of peculiar thoughts, he wondered, for example, why his wife, Georgina, was so fond of dogs? "She'd have been one of those women who thought that happiness was a warm puppy," he mused.

He, on the other hand, loathed the damned things; he much preferred cats because they kept themselves clean *and* buried their crap. "Happiness is definitely a warm pussy…" he sniggered.

True as that was, he wasn't getting much of it these days. Correction. He wasn't getting any. Georgina had just hit 50 and had become an instant oestrogen-free zone with zero libido. When he was ill, she had been a wonderful nurse, both tender and caring. He felt cherished and enjoyed the fuss she made of him when she massaged his aching body and plied him with honey and lemon drinks. Now that he was in recovery mode, their marriage had reverted to "normal": very little real intimacy, hardly any overt displays of affection, and if he hugged her, he could feel her stiffen. Intimate touching was taboo. He, on the other hand, still enjoyed kissing and cuddling, and some intimate fondling. He missed it, for Christ's sake!

At that point in his musings, he heard the swish of the shower curtain and saw his wife emerge dripping wet, draped in a towel. She picked up the hairdryer and aimed it at her dark hair.

"I heard what you were thinking," she called out above the noise of the dryer.

"What are you talking about? How can you possibly have *heard* what I was thinking?" he shouted above the din.

"We've been married long enough for me to know exactly what goes through your grubby little mind," she bellowed back.

She dropped the towel and stood in front of his face giving him an up-close view of her fanny as she played the dryer over it, teasing him with the sight and sound of her pubic hair rustling in the air flow. "How's that for a warm pussy, then? That's the last one you're going to see." And she grinned as she held the hairdryer over the bath and let it go.

Death of a Plumber

Vincent was sitting in the middle of the park bench, his arms outstretched along its back. He imagined he was flying. From this vantage point at the top of the slope near the park exit, he noticed an old lady struggling up the gradient towards him. Like so many homeless people, she was pushing a shopping trolley piled high with an odd mixture of junk she had probably picked up on her wanderings around town. Leaping to his feet, he rushed down to lend her a hand.

"Need any help?"

"That's very kind of you," she replied, "I would certainly be grateful for some assistance."

Far from living on the streets, she was on her way home. The trolley, which Vincent was now pushing, was crammed with a motley collection of the strangest things, including a small collapsible table, a rabbit, silk scarves, a top hat, and a host of other items he couldn't easily make out. Overcome by curiosity, he asked her what she did with it all.

"I'm a conjuror," she replied. "You probably find it hard to believe, but I've been practising magic for years. Nowadays, it's mostly kids' birthday parties. I'm on my way back from one right now. Years ago when I was much younger, I even had a stage show. How about you, young man? What do you do for a living?"

"Oh, I've got a boring office job. I'm on my lunch break at the moment and I've been trying to come up with a few ideas."

"What sort of ideas? For a new job?"

"Sort of. I realize it sounds ridiculous, but I've always wanted to be a writer. I've tried my hand at flash fiction, yet everything I send to publishers is rejected for the same reason: my 'characters are wooden and don't engage the reader'." He imitated the dismissive, lofty, tones of a busy editor.

"Oh, that's a shame," the old lady replied. "So what the publishers mean is you don't have the gift of bringing your characters to life?"

"I suppose so," he agreed.

By this time they had reached the old lady's home, at which point she turned to Vincent and said, quite out of the blue, "Don't worry, young man. In exchange for your kindness, I can bestow that gift upon you."

"Bestow that gift upon you," he mused, "Who the hell speaks like that?" Realizing now that she was one sandwich short of a picnic, Vincent thought he had better humour her:

"You mean you can turn me into one of those writers who make their characters come alive on the page?"

"Ye-es," she replied as she closed the door, "something like that."

"This old bird is batshit crazy," he muttered under his breath as he walked away.

*****

That evening, back home in his study, Vincent pondered what had happened. Perhaps he could turn the experience into a short story or flash fiction. When he sat down at his desk to make a start on it, he noticed a small pool of water next to his computer. He looked up to see a wet patch on the ceiling where a pipe must have sprung a leak.

"Damn it! I'll have to get hold of a plumber."

So, opening his laptop, Vincent typed "plumber" into the search engine. No sooner had he written the word than a plumber materialized next to him in his study and proceeded to fix the leak! So that was the nature of the old lady's "gift". It dawned on him that she must have heard what he said about her being crazy as he walked away from her door, and this was her revenge. She had effectively scuppered his ambitions of being a writer because it would now be impossible for him to write the name, trade, or profession of anyone on his laptop or in a notebook without those people springing up from nowhere in his tiny house or wherever he happened to be at the time.

"Oh, come on, think!" he said to himself, "there must be a way round this."

Then he had a brainwave. He waited for the plumber to finish mending the pipe and before he could ask for payment, Vincent deleted the word "plumber" from the screen, causing the man to vanish into thin air. Next, he typed "billionaire philanthropist" and sure enough one appeared next to him.

"How much do you need?" the billionaire asked.

"Oh, five million should be enough to be going on with," replied Vincent.

"No problem. Give me the number of your bank account and I'll make the transfer straightaway."

Once the operation had been completed and Vincent had checked his account, he deleted the billionaire just as he had done with the plumber.

"And now for some real fun," thought Vincent and, grinning broadly, he typed:

"Beautiful young blonde nymphomaniac" ...

The Dwarf

Part I

My ground floor apartment overlooks the condo courtyard and the street beyond. A lady, maybe in her mid-thirties, regularly parks her shiny new car nearby and proceeds to walk a large Dalmatian past the condo on her way around the neighbourhood. The lady in question is a dwarf. She presents all the characteristics of disproportionate dwarfism: short limbs, large buttocks, a prominent forehead, and a rolling gait. We have only ever coincided on a couple of occasions outside on the street. Each time, we exchanged the usual pleasantries, and she went on her way, and I on mine.

I often think how difficult it must be for her, how she probably had a miserable childhood because other children can be so cruel towards anyone who looks different. Thinking back, I remembered a number of dwarves I had known personally, like a journalist in Salamanca many years ago, but he had the advantage, if it can be described as such, of being a proportionate dwarf. He looked much the same as everyone else except that he was very short. However, all the other dwarves I'd seen were of the disproportionate type like my lady neighbour and they tended to perform in circuses or other spectacles, such as mock bullfights.

One day as I was walking around town, I saw the dwarf lady without her dog, surrounded by half a dozen teenage boys who were clearly harassing her. They might say that they were just teasing her, but they were being deliberately nasty. You can imagine the kind of thing, I'm sure: "Where's Snow White, then?" or "Which one are you? Dopey? When do the other six arrive?" Now, I'm an old man. In fact I was born the same year that the film of *Snow White and the Seven Dwarves* was first screened. Yet, despite my age, I couldn't ignore what was going on so, I walked up to the gang of spotty-faced young thugs and pointedly asked them what they thought they were doing. "Run along grandad or you might get hurt," the biggest and most aggressive one growled.

Because of my age and because running across cocky goons like this bunch on the lookout for trouble is inevitable, I always carry a 30cm steel rod in my shoulder bag. A sharp smack across the wrists or fingers would quickly deter aggression as would a poke in the groin with it. I was just about to pull it out of my bag, when the dwarf lady said, "Don't worry. I can handle this."

She turned to the galoot who had threatened me and said sweetly, “How’s your acne coming along, sonny? Do you really think it can’t get any worse? Not heard of the monkeypox virus, then?” And with that she pointed at his face, which immediately burst into a florid, bubbling mass of suppurating pustules! It was all I could do to see where his eyes were! The other five teenagers turned pale and took to their heels terrified that the same thing would happen to them.

“Thanks for being a gentleman and intervening on my behalf, but as you can see, I’m able to take care of myself. And I don’t actually need my dog to protect me. I just like dogs. My name is Griselda, by the way, and I run my own online magic business. Would you like my app?”

The Dwarf

Part II

The following story was difficult for me to write, both physically and emotionally, as will eventually become apparent.

It all goes back to when I wrote a short piece about a dwarf lady that I had seen from my apartment window when she was walking her dog. Even though I had never talked to her, I invented a tale about her. It was an attempt to show sympathy for her condition while attributing magical powers to her. Subsequently, I found my mind dwelling on the dwarf lady almost to the point of obsession, wondering what she was really like, what she did for a living, how long she had been living around here and who her friends were. Then one day, just as I was coming out of the gate of the condo, there she was, waiting with her dog by her car while a badly parked van moved so that she could get into her car and drive off somewhere.

As I had recently published the little tale inspired by her, I was especially keen to engage her in conversation, something that had happened so far only in my imagination. Her dog, a Dalmatian, was the obvious way into initiating such a chat. "Hello, I suppose the other hundred are at home," I quipped. She smiled and replied, "You bet. And they keep me pretty busy." She had a pleasantly modulated voice, and radiated friendliness. "I've spotted you a few times from my window. Do you live nearby?" I asked. "Yes, in that street," she said pointing down the road. As we chatted, I let slip that I dabbled in writing, producing the occasional very odd short story as a way of staying sane during the pandemic. She looked a little surprised but said it sounded like a great coping mechanism. Our brief but affable exchange came to an end when the van driver finally moved off allowing her to put the dog in the back of the car and then drive off.

Our paths didn't cross again for about a month. We met by chance on the edge of our neighbourhood where, as usual, she was walking her dog. I greeted her cheerfully, asking her how she was. Her reaction was far from friendly, though, nothing at all like the first time we had spoken. She was quite prickly, in fact.

"Everything alright?" I asked.

"Not really," she snapped. "Do you remember telling me that you dabbled in writing? You mentioned that you wrote, and I quote, 'the occasional very odd short story'." Her tone was tetchy. "Ye-es," I replied. "Well, I have a friend who's a great fan of online literature sites and he came across a short story called **The Dwarf** that was apparently written by you. And he was not in the least amused by it and now that I've read it, nor am I."

"I'm sorry," I replied, "I really thought it was sympathetic to you and your condition."

"There you go again! That's the point! I don't need your sympathy or your drawing attention to 'my condition' as you put it by describing it in such detail. You've got the same underlying prejudices as everybody else. As for that nonsense about me having magical powers. What a load of crap that is! It emphasizes the fact that you have the same fantasies about people like me as narrated in fairy tales!"

I was so embarrassed that I could feel myself shrinking with shame. "It was just a story, a fiction," I mumbled. "I didn't mean to offend you." As I spoke, I looked into her eyes, and it dawned on me that mine were now on the same level as hers ... The next minute, I was looking at her knees! "What's happening to me?" I screamed.

"Don't ask me. This is *your* story," and she chuckled as she walked away.

The Irony of Noir

"Home, sweet home," Aubrey whooped "and I've got it all to myself! Yippee!"

His parents had just set off to join the ship that would take them on a three-month cruise around the Mediterranean and he was delighted to have the house to himself during that time. He had plans, you see. But first things first. He'd applied to Oxford University and was fully expecting to receive an invitation to an interview because he had been the star pupil at his boarding school.

A few days after his parents had departed, the longed-for letter inviting him for an interview arrived. He was keen to read English Literature at university, mainly because he'd always nursed an ambition to be a writer himself. He was a particularly avid reader of the noir genre. Aubrey fantasised about being another Edgar Allan Poe or Raymond Chandler or, at the very least, a writer cast in the same mould as the Roald Dahl of "Tales of the Unexpected." He'd even concocted some noir themes for a series of parties that he intended to throw for friends while he had the grand old family home to himself...

On the day before the interview, as he left the house to set off to catch the train to Oxford, he "touched wood" for luck by dragging his left hand along the neighbour's fence. As he did so, he felt a sharp pain. A rusty nail that had been hammered through the fence from the other side had cut his palm. Since the scratch didn't hurt too much, he simply wrapped a handkerchief round it to stop the bleeding and hurried on down to the station.

The interview seemed to go well the next day. The Admissions Tutor was friendly—he even enquired about Aubrey's now bandaged hand—and, as far as he could tell, appeared impressed by the performance of the aspiring student, particularly when he delivered an insightful analysis of his favourite noir writers.

"You should receive our decision next week in the post," the tutor said as he showed the young man out, "and I do hope your hand gets better soon."

On the same day that the good news arrived—for he had indeed been offered a place—he began to experience a slight fever and a general feeling of fatigue.

"What a time to catch a bug," he thought, "just as Christmas is around the corner. Well, after a couple of days in bed I'll be as right as rain and then I can plan the first noir party." He was really looking forward to it.

However, getting better took longer than he expected. He'd spent two weeks under the covers, getting up only to make himself a sandwich or a bowl of soup, but by the middle of the third week, he didn't have the strength to get out of bed at all, while the wound on his hand was looking decidedly ugly. The worst of it was that the battery in his cell phone had run out and the charger was downstairs in the kitchen, which meant he couldn't ring the doctor. Being "home alone" was not turning out to be so much fun after all.

So, he lay there reviewing his symptoms: his limbs were still aching, and he'd begun to suffer palpitations. He also noticed red patches on both arms. He assumed he must have bruised himself while tossing and turning in bed. What he didn't realize was that they were actually signs of blood poisoning—not being a science student has its disadvantages, you see. Next, he became aware of something that was really unusual: it dawned on him that he hadn't passed water for at least two days. Not long after that, he went into septic shock, suffered heart failure, and died.

Presumably, his funeral will take place when his parents get back home from their cruise. Touch wood.

HRT

"Hi, Brittany!" said Marie-France. "Gosh, it's been ages since we last met! The last time we saw each other you looked so down in the dumps. Now, you look radiant!"

"Oh, the reason for that is that I finally divorced that slob, Boris. I don't know how I put up with the pig for so many years, what with his drunkenness and affairs. God knows what other women actually saw in him. He was such a bloody awful wreck of a man and useless in bed as in everything else. You can't imagine the relief of ridding myself of him."

"Well, good for you. I often wondered why you married the hulking brute. Have you met somebody else or are you just enjoying the freedom of being a bachelor girl again?" asked Marie-France.

"I did live on my own for a while, but I found being a singleton overrated, especially when I met François. He's such an incredible man, so attentive and understanding and that accent… Ooh! On top of which he's a brilliant chef with a Michelin star to his name! As you might imagine, I found him irresistible and when he asked me to marry him, I leapt at the chance although I was a little worried about the sexual side of our marriage because my libido had all but vanished after ten years of going to bed with Boris. However, I discovered that HRT works wonders. François is so exciting and satisfying in bed!"

"Oh, so hormone replacement therapy really works then?"

"Who said anything about hormone replacement therapy? I'm talking about *husband* replacement therapy! That's what works. I can thoroughly recommend it."

Daisies and Mallows

I was watering the lawn when the gate opened and Ben, who had lived next door ten years ago, greeted me with a wave.

"Hello, Geoff. Still gardening, I see!" and he grinned, "How's the wife?"

"Oh, you know *her*: Mia, by name, MIA by nature!" I laughed.

"What do you mean by that?" he asked, surprised.

"Just my little joke. She's gone I'm afraid."

"Gone? Gone where? Are you two separated, then?"

"You could say that, I suppose, but what I really mean is that she's snuffed it. In short, she's dead."

"Good heavens! You don't seem very upset. What did she die of?"

"Well, to avoid the C-word, let's call it '*crabbiness'*."

My friend couldn't believe his ears. His jaw dropped in utter disbelief.

"Come on, man!" I retorted. "It's no big deal, we all have to go some time. She just went a bit earlier than some others… As a matter of fact, I've buried her in the garden. All legal and above board, or rather, ahem, below ground. I just wanted to keep her close."

"You do seem more than a bit offhand about it all. You don't seem bothered in the slightest."

"Well, people do tend to pussyfoot around talking about death. The language is either terribly sombre and mournful or it gives rise to a light-hearted kind of black humour. You know, like talking about people 'pushing up the daisies'. It seems that we Brits aren't the only ones to have expressions like that. Did you know that the Spanish refer to the dead as 'growing mallows' while the French have them 'eating the roots of dandelions!' And the stolid Germans regard their dead as 'gazing at radishes from below'. How weird is that?"

My friend cast his eyes around the garden in search of such plants. Finally, he remarked, "Well I don't see any daisies or mallows in your garden, and there's certainly no sign of dandelions or radishes. In fact the only plant that seems to be thriving here is that poison ivy covering the garden wall..."

Homophone

I'm the right-hand man of a gay gangland boss. He has an ornate pink telephone in his office, which he jocularly refers to as his 'homophone'. As you can tell, the boss has a sense of humour as well as an interest in things linguistic and for this reason he hired a phonetician as his messenger boy. However, the hiring turned out to be a mistake and today the phonetician is to be eliminated.

So here we are, the phonetician and I and a couple of henchmen, on the boss's yacht in the middle of the bay. The victim is pale and shaking as he realizes what is about to befall him, although he can't understand why.

"The boss has always liked me, especially the way I look," he pleaded. "Only this morning I heard him say: 'That phonetician, what a waist!'"

"I'm afraid you're wrong," I muttered. "What he actually said was: 'That phonetician, what a waste!' You, dear boy, were supposed to convey his messages with clarity, like when he told you to waive Bugsy Malone's death sentence, in the presence of the enforcer."

"But I did," whimpered the phonetician. I sighed. "No you didn't, you dumb pillock. You *waved* the death sentence in front of the enforcer, who then shot poor Bugsy dead. That's why you're on this boat in the middle of the bay."

"But I heard the boss talking down the phone to you and he distinctly said, 'Wait and see'," the phonetician replied desperately.

"That's the trouble with you phoneticians. You see everything in phonetic symbols. If only you could learn to write like other people, you might not be in this mess. What he actually said was: 'Weight and sea'. It was shorthand, so to speak, for 'Fit the phonetician with concrete boots and throw him over the side'. Why do you think the boss calls his phone a homophone?"

Splash!

Home Sweet Home

"How could you think of doing such a thing?"

Mildred was appalled that her son, Percy, had suggested that she should move into a care home and had taken her to see one, much against her will. At 72, she was perfectly compos mentis. After all, she was still able to code computer programs, having run her own successful IT business since she was thirty years old. The profits had enabled her to buy an enormous country house in a sought-after part of the county and she was now very well-provided for by her handsome pension plan. She was certainly in no mood to leave her own home.

Her son, on the other hand, was a feckless sponger, a confirmed bachelor who had been living off his mother since the day he was born. He had failed at whatever he had turned his hand to. And she was damned sure he was going to fail at dumping her in a care home.

"You'll love it here," he wheedled as he showed her round the E.G. Sunset Home for the Elderly, "and I'll visit you regularly, don't worry."

"What does the E.G. stand for? Elephants' Graveyard?" she snapped.

"No mother, it stands for European Group. The firm runs a number of such homes around the county as well as abroad."

"But just look at the people in here! Talk about dried arrangements! I'm not gaga, thank you very much, and have no intention of going along with your idea and that's that!"

So, Percy had no option but to drive his mother back home to her country pile. Once she got there, Mildred set about dealing with the 'Percy problem'. It was obvious to her that his intention all along had been to shuffle her out of the way so that he could then apply for power of attorney on the grounds that his mother was no longer capable of coping with her affairs. The cheek of the man!

"Well, we'll see about that," fumed Mildred. As her entire career had been in IT, in no time at all she had hacked into various bank accounts belonging to people that neither she nor Percy knew and siphoned off copious amounts of their money into the account that she had set up for Percy's allowance years before. She made it look as if those people had invested in a Ponzi scheme run by her son. She also made sure that the digital trail would lead back to Percy's computer.

Within a week, the cyber police had hunted Percy down and hauled him off to the police cells where he was held on remand until his case came up. His 'shocked' mother refused to pay for an expensive lawyer for her wayward son. Percy had to make do with a wet-behind-the-ears pro bono junior lawyer who turned out to be as inept as his client, who was eventually sentenced to 10 years in prison for robbery and fraud.

"Don't worry," smiled Mildred at the end of the trial, "I'll visit you regularly."

Extraordinary General Meeting of the Four Horsemen of the Apocalypse

Chairperson: Death

Members of the Board:

War, Famine and Pestilence

Death glowered at the other three board members and did not mince his words as he opened the session:

"I've convened this meeting because you three sons of bitches are working **me** to death! In the good old days my main task was dealing with those who met their Maker through natural causes. You know, old age, heart attacks and so on. OK, so you three contributed with the odd famine or a bit of smallpox, the so-called ingredient X to spice up the death rate. Even a skirmish or two like the Thirty Years War, not to mention the Hundred Years War. Mind you, WWI was a bit over the top, and WWII ended with a big bang that provided me with plenty of freaking overtime, but nothing I couldn't handle at that point. However,..."

"Now, hang on a minute. Just quit beefing, will you!" Famine interrupted. "My involvement in your life, or should I say Death, has generally been fairly minimal. We know all about the lean years in ancient Egypt and people going hungry in the Middle Ages and so on. But it's not my fault that humans breed like rabbits so that there's not enough food for everybody. In my younger days, I used to roam across Egypt, Ethiopia, Nigeria, and perhaps South Sudan periodically and that was more or less it. But nobody could cater—no pun intended, he smirked—for someone like Stalin who imposed Holodomor on Soviet Ukraine, and I didn't encourage his clone Putin to do something similar in today's Ukraine either."

"Stop passing the buck!" growled Death. "Food banks are cropping up everywhere, even in supposedly rich countries like the UK. When kids say they're famished these days they damned well mean it! On top of that, Pestilence has had a field day with Covid-19. And then he had the nerve to come up with the bright idea of monkey pox! I ask you! You couldn't make it up. Why not just stick to bubonic plague or even a touch of Ebola??"

"Don't give me a hard time!" Pestilence chimed in. "You don't really believe my little ailments spring up spontaneously, do you? If you think about it, **War** is at the root of most of these problems because my colleague, Famine, and I inevitably follow in his wake—again, no pun intended. That's why he's got you, dear Death, as number one on his speed dial. War's destruction of a country's infrastructure like hospitals and science laboratories enables disease to become rampant. So don't blame **me**. You need to have a word with War. By the way, have you ever wondered how he ended up with a horse in the first place? The rest of us are, in one way or another, forces of nature. The vicissitudes of the climate on the one hand and creatures of every kind living cheek by jowl on the other are bound to give rise to Famine, Pestilence and Death, but War doesn't seem to be in quite the same category. War is very much more of a human invention."

All eyes turned towards the last named, who was lounging nonchalantly, his feet up on the table and picking his teeth with a stiletto. Death glared at War and rasped, "What have you got to say in your defence?"

War stuck the stiletto in the tabletop, pulled his feet off the table, heaved a sigh, and said, "Hold your horses! Just back off. What you say is only partly true. I **am** actually a natural feature of the entire animal kingdom, which includes humans, of course. You must all be well aware that for humans I am what they call 'an extension of politics by other means'. Once politicians become obsessed with dreams of empire and go in search of the Earth's dwindling resources, they invite me along as back-up. The animal kingdom is red in tooth and claw, right? Like young lions forcing out the old ones or hyenas chasing down the weak. I'm in the genes of every living creature... until they're not!" and he laughed out loud. "If 'Make love not war' had any traction, there would be a fifth horseman, but there isn't. You only have to read the so-called social media to realize that trolls and mischief-makers far outnumber the kind-hearted in this world. Just think of the 40,000+ Americans a year who gun each other down, meaning that even at the individual level you have mini wars, that is, murders, mass murders even. I have the feeling that you three, but particularly that ghoul, Death, would like to kill **me** off, but he can't because I'm immortal, at least until the planet wipes out the human race, which, to be sure, is in the offing—no pun intended there either, even though I'm the one who put the laughter into slaughter!"

Death looked even more depressed.

"Oh, come on, cheer up," Pestilence piped up. "You must have noticed that I toned down the virulence of Covid in its later variants, which means that not as many will need you in attendance quite so soon. At least, you'll have time to get **your** breath back," he tittered, "and monkey pox is actually more irritating than deadly."

"True enough," Famine wheezed, "and don't forget, dear Death, as you go around reducing the number of people on the planet, there'll be more to eat for those who are left, won't there? So, to quote Monty Python, always look on the bright side of life!"

Death was not wholly convinced or cheered by these reassurances. Nonetheless, once he had persuaded the others to increase his bonus for more than meeting his targets and to provide a couple of extra horses to alleviate the burden on the pale old nag he had been riding since time immemorial, he brought the meeting to a close and signed the minutes, aka the human race's Death warrant.

Shogun

Joe 'Shogun' Lombardo was the fruit of a brief liaison between a Japanese American girl and a drifter of Italian stock in the 1950s. Despite this inauspicious start in life, he went on to become a successful businessman working for a large conglomerate. Recently retired, he was looking for some domestic help, so he put an advertisement in the local paper:

Young Housekeeper Required
Excellent Pay and Conditions.
Applicants should send CVs
including cellphone number
and photo by email to jsl@gmail.com

His advertisement prompted a flurry of replies. Seventy-year-old Joe Lombardo devoted an evening to sifting through all 55 of them, eventually picking just one to interview: an attractive 28-year-old brunettc.

When Julia arrived at the smart address, she was greeted by a well-preserved, broad-shouldered, silver-haired man with slightly oriental features.

"Good morning, and thank you for coming, Julia."

"Thank you for inviting me," she replied. "Believe me, I really need this job. Times are hard and I'm willing to do anything to find work." She smiled, hitching her mini skirt up further.

"Well, that's good to know, but I assure you that you won't have to do anything that demeans you."

"I must say you have a lovely home. I've never been in such a large house. It's the sort of home I've always dreamed of," she sighed. "You have such wonderful taste," she went on, looking around at the furniture and ornaments.

"That's very nice of you. I bought this place some time ago when the neighborhood was being developed. At the time, it was quite exclusive, but recently there have been a number of home invasions around here, which is why I had a couple security cameras installed at the front."

"That must be worrying," Julia chimed in.

"All those expensive ornaments you see were picked up on my travels. I spent my working life traveling on business. Now, I hardly go out and have everything delivered but what I need is some company. That's why I advertised for a housekeeper."

"I can understand that. Loneliness is so often a problem for the elderly," she responded, hoping her voice sounded compassionate.

"Let's get down to business then," he smiled. "The job involves keeping the house clean, making me meals, so that I don't have to rely on pizza deliveries," he laughed, "and some light administrative duties. It's a live-in post, in other words."

"That's fine by me," said Julia.

He smiled again. "You would have your own room with ensuite bathroom and a day and a half off each week. Your monthly salary would be as stated in this envelope. If you prefer cash in hand, that can be arranged."

"Sounds OK," she commented as she began to tear the envelope open. When she saw the figure inside, she could hardly believe her eyes.

"Will you take the job?" he asked.

"You bet I will! I'll start tomorrow morning."

"Wonderful. Here are the keys to the door and the alarm code. Please memorize it and destroy the paper. We can't be too careful."

"I noticed you have a huge back garden. The lawn and the flowerbeds look a little neglected, though, if you don't mind me saying. If you like, my boyfriend could do the gardening," she offered. "It wouldn't cost anything because what you're paying me is incredibly generous."

"OK. Bring him with you tomorrow and I'll show him where to find the tools and hosepipe."

******

When Julia returned to the trailer home where she lived with the shiftless Carter, she bounced up and down with excitement. She couldn't believe her good fortune.

"You should see his home! He must be loaded. Just look at what he's prepared to pay me, for Chrissake, and in cash if I like! A guy who can pay out cash like that when he hardly goes out must have a stash at home. Listen, you're gonna do the gardening so you can case the place."

Julia moved into Lombardo's house the next day and introduced Carter, who was as impressed as Julia.

Shogun greeted them, saying, "You can have the run of the house except for my office. That's my inner sanctum and is out of bounds." He turned to Carter. "I don't mind you stopping over occasionally since Julia has to live in and you two are in a relationship. You're both welcome to use the pool in the basement. I look forward to having you around."

Carter was an ignorant philistine, but even he was impressed by the lavishly appointed house and the exotic figurines and artefacts from all the places Lombardo had visited on his travels.

One day, after Julia and Carter had showered together and were back in her bedroom, she whispered to him, "It would be dead easy to suffocate him in his sleep, break into his office and clean it out. We could make it look like a home invasion."

That very night, they crept up the stairs and made their way on tiptoe to Joe's bedroom door. Carter eased it open. Two blasts from a shotgun blew them away.

What neither of them had realized was that Lombardo's outside security cameras had picked up the couple on several occasions over a period of weeks lurking around the homes in the area. He had come to the conclusion that they were casing the homes and were most likely the ones responsible for the spate of recent burglaries. Ever since Julia had taken the job, Lombardo had been monitoring their every move and conversation. Apart from the exterior cameras, he had others all over the house hidden in the figurines and artefacts that he had collected from his travels and spent hours checking recordings in his inner sanctum.

More to the point, neither of them had understood that the 'business conglomerate' that he had worked for was the Mafia... And you can guess why he was nicknamed 'Shogun'.

Acknowledgements

The Grave's a Fine and Private Place first published online at Literally Stories

The Snuffing Machine first published in print in Otherwise Engaged

Cats and Dogs first published in print by Pure Slush

Death of a Plumber first published online at Lothlorien Poetry Journal

The Dwarf Parts I and II first published online by Syndic Literary Journal

The Irony of Noir first published in print by Otherwise Engaged

HRT first published online at Syndic Literary Journal

Homophone first published online at Lothlorien Poetry Journal

ISBN: 978-81-19654-93-2

First Edition: 2023
Rs. 200/-

Cyberwit.net
HIG 45 Kaushambi Kunj, Kalindipuram
Allahabad - 211011 (U.P.) India
http://www.cyberwit.net
Tel: +(91) 9415091004
E-mail: info@cyberwit.net

Printed at Repro.

www.ingramcontent.com/pod-product-compliance
Lightning Source LLC
LaVergne TN
LVHW091238150826
845673LV00003B/1206

* 9 7 8 8 1 1 9 6 5 4 9 3 2 *